W9-CIP-971

Bannockburn School Dist. 106
2165 Telegraph Road
Bannockburn, Illinois 60015

DATE DUE

FOLLETT

TOMÁS AND
THE LIBRARY LADY

PAT MORA · ILLUSTRATED BY RAUL COLÓN

DRAGONFLY BOOKS® ALFRED A. KNOPF · NEW YORK

DRAGONFLY BOOKS® PUBLISHED BY ALFRED A. KNOPF, INC.

www.randomhouse.com/kids

Library of Congress Cataloging-in-Publication Data

Mora, Pat.
Tomás and the library lady / by Pat Mora ; illustrated by Raul Colón
p.   cm.
Summary: While helping his family in their work as migrant laborers far from their home, Tomás
finds an entire world to explore in the books at the public library.
[1. Books and reading—Fiction. 2. Librarians—Fiction. 3. Migrant labor—Fiction. 4. Mexican
Americans—Fiction.] I. Colón, Raul, ill. II. Title.
PZ7.M78819To   1997
[E]—dc20   89-37490

ISBN 0-679-80401-3 (trade)
0-679-90401-8 (lib. bdg.)
0-679-94173-8 (Span. lib. bdg.)
0-679-84173-3 (Span. pbk.)
0-375-80349-1 (pbk.)

First Dragonfly Books® edition: February 2000

Printed in the United States of America
20 19 18 17 16 15 14 13 12

DRAGONFLY BOOKS and colophon, KNOPF, and BORZOI BOOKS
are registered trademarks of Random House, Inc.

*In memory of Tomás Rivera, who loved books,
and for librarians who lure us in*
—P. M.

For Sylvia and Carl
—R. C.

It was midnight. The light of the full moon followed the tired old car. Tomás was tired too. Hot and tired. He missed his own bed, in his own house in Texas.

Tomás was on his way to Iowa again with his family. His mother and father were farm workers. They picked fruit and vegetables for Texas farmers in the winter and for Iowa farmers in the summer. Year after year they bump-bumped along in their rusty old car. "Mamá," whispered Tomás, "if I had a glass of cold water, I would drink it in large gulps. I would suck the ice. I would pour the last drops of water on my face."

Tomás was glad when the car finally stopped. He helped his grandfather, Papá Grande, climb down. Tomás said, *"Buenas noches"*–"Good night"–to Papá, Mamá, Papá Grande, and to his little brother, Enrique. He curled up on the cot in the small house that his family shared with the other workers.

Early the next morning Mamá and Papá went out to pick corn in the green fields. All day they worked in the hot sun. Tomás and Enrique carried water to them. Then the boys played with a ball Mamá had sewn from an old teddy bear.

When they got hot, they sat under a tree with Papá Grande. "Tell us the story about the man in the forest," said Tomás.

Tomás liked to listen to Papá Grande tell stories in Spanish. Papá Grande was the best storyteller in the family.

"*En un tiempo pasado,*" Papá Grande began. "Once upon a time . . . on a windy night a man was riding a horse through a forest. The wind was howling, *whoooooooooo*, and the leaves were blowing, *whish, whish* . . .

"All of a sudden something grabbed the man. He couldn't move. He was too scared to look around. All night long he wanted to ride away. But he couldn't.

"How the wind howled, *whoooooooooo*. How the leaves blew. How his teeth chattered!

"Finally the sun came up. Slowly the man turned around. And who do you think was holding him?"

Tomás smiled and said, "A thorny tree."

Papá Grande laughed. "Tomás, you know all my stories," he said. "There are many more in the library. You are big enough to go by yourself. Then you can teach us new stories."

The next morning Tomás walked downtown. He looked at the big library. Its tall windows were like eyes glaring at him. Tomás walked around and around the big building. He saw children coming out carrying books. Slowly he started climbing up, up the steps. He counted them to himself in Spanish. *Uno, dos, tres, cuatro* . . . His mouth felt full of cotton.

Tomás stood in front of the library doors. He pressed his nose against the glass and peeked in. The library was huge!

A hand tapped his shoulder. Tomás jumped. A tall lady looked down at him. "It's a hot day," she said. "Come inside and have a drink of water. What's your name?" she asked.

"Tomás," he said.

"Come, Tomás," she said.

Inside it was cool. Tomás had never seen so many books. The lady watched him. "Come," she said again, leading him to a drinking fountain. "First some water. Then I will bring books to this table for you. What would you like to read about?"

"Tigers. Dinosaurs," said Tomás.

Tomás drank the cold water. He looked at the tall ceiling. He looked at all the books around the room. He watched the lady take some books from the shelves and bring them to the table. "This chair is for you, Tomás," she said. Tomás sat down. Then very carefully he took a book from the pile and opened it.

Tomás saw dinosaurs bending their long necks to lap shiny water. He heard the cries of a wild snake-bird. He felt the warm neck of the dinosaur as he held on tight for a ride. Tomás forgot about the library lady. He forgot about Iowa and Texas.

"Tomás, Tomás," said the library lady softly. Tomás looked around. The library was empty. The sun was setting.

The library lady looked at Tomás for a long time. She said, "Tomás, would you like to borrow two library books? I will check them out in my name."

Tomás walked out of the library carrying his books. He ran home, eager to show the new stories to his family.

Papá Grande looked at the library books. "Read to me," he said to Tomás. First Tomás showed him the pictures. He pointed to the tiger. "*¡Qué tigre tan grande!*" Tomás said first in Spanish and then in English, "What a big tiger!"

"Read to me in English," said Papá Grande. Tomás read about tiger eyes shining brightly in the jungle at night. He roared like a huge tiger. Papá, Mamá, and Enrique laughed. They came and sat near him to hear his story.

Some days Tomás went with his parents to the town dump.
They looked for pieces of iron to sell. Enrique looked for toys.
Tomás looked for books. He would put the books in the sun to
bake away the smell.

All summer, whenever he could, Tomás went to the library. The library lady would say, "First a drink of water and then some new books, Tomás."

On quiet days the library lady said, "Come to my desk and read to me, Tomás." Then she would say, "Please teach me some new words in Spanish."

Tomás would smile. He liked being the teacher. The library lady pointed to a book. "Book is *libro*," said Tomás.

"*Libro*," said the library lady.

"*Pájaro*," said Tomás, flapping his arms.

The library lady laughed. "Bird," she said.

On days when the library was busy, Tomás read to himself. He'd look at the pictures for a long time. He smelled the smoke at an Indian camp. He rode a black horse across a hot, dusty desert. And in the evenings he would read the stories to Mamá, Papá, Papá Grande, and Enrique.

One August afternoon Tomás brought Papá Grande to the library.

The library lady said, *"Buenas tardes, señor."* Tomás smiled. He had taught the library lady how to say "Good afternoon, sir" in Spanish.

"Buenas tardes, señora," Papá Grande replied.

Softly Tomás said, "I have a sad word to teach you today. The word is *adiós*. It means good-bye."

Tomás was going back to Texas. He would miss this quiet place, the cool water, the many books. He would miss the library lady.

"My mother sent this to thank you," said Tomás, handing her a small package. "It is *pan dulce*, sweet bread. My mother makes the best *pan dulce* in Texas."

The library lady said, "How nice. How very nice. *Gracias*, Tomás. Thank you." She gave Tomás a big hug.

That night, bumping along again in the tired old car, Tomás held a shiny new book, a present from the library lady. Papá Grande smiled and said, "More stories for the new storyteller."

Tomás closed his eyes. He saw the dinosaurs drinking cool water long ago. He heard the cry of the wild snakebird. He felt the warm neck of the dinosaur as he held on tight for a bumpy ride.

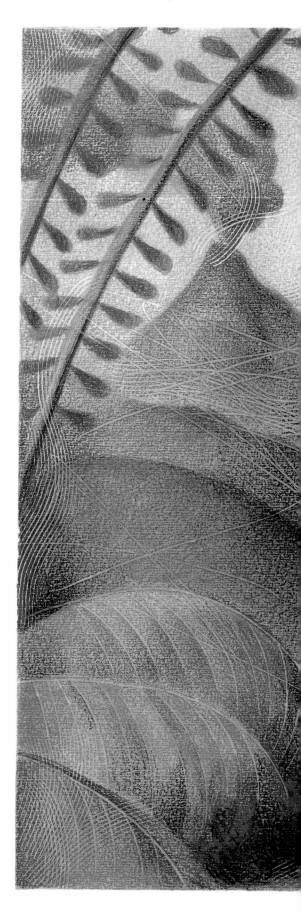

A Note About the Story

Tomás Rivera was born in Crystal City, Texas, in 1935. A migrant worker who valued education, Tomás Rivera became a writer, a professor, a university administrator, and a national education leader. When Dr. Rivera died in 1984, he was the chancellor of the University of California at Riverside. The campus library now bears the name of the boy who was encouraged to read by a librarian in Iowa.